Finger Food

Published by Accent Press Ltd – 2012

ISBN 9781908192929

The Quick Reads project in Wales is a joint venture between the Welsh Government and the Welsh Books Council.

Printed and boundby CPI Group (UK) Ltd, Croydon, CR0 4YY

Cover design by Joelle Brindley

CYNGOR LLYFRAU CYMRU
WELSH BOOKS COUNCIL

Noddir gan
Lywodraeth Cymru
Sponsored by
Welsh Government

Finger Food

Helen Lederer

ACCENT PRESS LTD

Chapter One

Bella knew the signs of stress. The tight feeling across her chest, her pulse racing so fast she could feel it in her neck. And this morning there was something new. A tic by her eye.

On the other end of the phone, Sharon at Flair 4 Living TV seemed to take too much pleasure in saying, 'I'm afraid Yvonne's in a meeting at the moment, Bella. But I'll just go and check.'

Then came the added insult of having to listen to a mix of James Bond themes for five long minutes before the receptionist returned. This time her voice was full of fake regret.

'Shame! You've just missed her, Bella! Try again tomorrow perhaps?'

'I certainly will, Sharon.' Bella forced a smile into her voice but had to keep the phone under her ear. She had no spare hands to end the call – what with holding her umbrella, the phone, her newspaper and her small handbag. She thought she could hear Sharon chuckling as she fumbled to disconnect. Cow.

Bella shook the rain off her umbrella. She had been phoning her old boss Yvonne daily for the last six months. If she couldn't get her old job back she might at least be annoying.

Bella preferred to tell people she had been 'let go' rather than sacked from her job as researcher at Flair 4 Living daytime TV channel because it sounded better. She had spent years working at the channel, chopping vegetables, wiping surfaces and coming up with some great ideas. One had been called 'When Vicars Attack!' which was turned down, as was the one called 'How Clean is your Nostril Hair?' as well as 'Ready Steady Cheese'. In fact they'd all been rejected almost immediately. But Bella was not put off. At the back of her mind was the dream that one day she would be invited to present her own show. She just needed to come up with the right idea. One that was more food-focussed.

Unfortunately, Flair 4 Living's controller Yvonne did not agree. On the day of her sacking Bella had presented her brilliant proposal of a new pilot idea. 'Finger Food' was to be a low-brow digital-TV food and chat programme. After an hour of pitching the idea, Bella had gone home with the quiet confidence that this show

2

would be taken up. And she would be cast as the presenter she had always dreamed of being.

Instead, Yvonne had personally dropped a letter through her letter box only hours later, saying that 'due to various changes at the channel' Bella would have to be 'sacrificed'. While they 'valued her ability to develop ideas and respected her talent as a "stand-in presenter", with a particular skill for table displays, they'd have to let her go'. Yvonne added she was 'so sorry to say goodbye to Bella, especially as they "went back"'. (They'd been at Guides together a long time ago.) Bella knew that of course Yvonne wasn't sorry at all. In fact she sounded pleased to have finally got rid of her.

Ever since then Bella had been trying to make sense of her life as an unemployed person and had even bought a self-help book called *Making Sense of Being Sacked*. This gave instructions on how to get out of bed in the morning to avoid 'moping' (jumping was one idea), how to talk to at least one person a day (this could include a policeman) and how to have a vision of something nice in one's mind (pretending to be on a date with George Clooney was offered as a helpful example). So Bella had created a new routine. She would leave the house at 8.30 a.m., walk to the newsagent to buy a newspaper and then walk to the local cake shop. The cake-shop visit she did every day except Sundays because that was the owner's late start. She didn't buy women's magazines to read because the recipes made her upset and irritable. They weren't up to her high standards. Bella loved food. She loved arranging it, talking about it, eating it and making table displays to show it off. This was her passion and when she had no outlets for it she was lost. And hungry.

Still juggling her bag and umbrella she kicked open the door of Carmel's Cake Emporium and felt a wave of relief wash over her. Out of the rain and in range of cake she was safe.

The rain had plastered her pudding-cut hairstyle to her face, giving her the look of a wet seal. Her eyeliner had leaked on to her over-rouged cheeks and her streaked highlights were sadly now almost as dark as the rest of her hair. Bella caught a glimpse of herself in the mirrored cake counter and wished she hadn't. She released the tight belt of her old raincoat (Harrods sale) from around her largish middle and was pleased to note that at least the new floral smock top (Top Shop) and khaki three-quarter trousers had survived the dampness. She hadn't been sure about the trousers. They had slightly annoying ties around the hems. And after months of cake-eating they were also getting a bit snug 'around the la la', as Sharon would say. But they could pass as stylish leisure wear on a budget, which was the look she was adopting.

Bella tapped her fingers on the counter to make sure Carmel knew she was hungry and that she was there. She could see Carmel's back in the inner kitchenette area, shaking with the effort of buttering another customer's scones.

Bella coughed. She wanted to say 'Hurry up, Carmel. I'm very depressed. I need cake urgently'. Instead she called out a casual, 'Morning!' trying to make the single word sound bold and important. Surely Carmel would understand the urgency of serving her rather than some other less needy customer who'd had the bad manners to order scones?

Bella turned to view the rest of the tea room, checking if her usual seat was vacant. She hoped she hadn't left it too late. Ever since she'd got sacked, Bella had become more superstitious and a bit obsessive. It was taking her longer and longer to get out of the house. She'd checked the light switch five times that day, which was one more time than the day before.

There was one other customer, seated in the corner. An old lady who must have ordered the scones.

Bella was in luck. The window seat was vacant. From there, she'd have a clear view of The Dress, still shimmering and glinting across the road in the window of Bride 2 B. This was no ordinary dress. It was not an A-line everyday shift dress that you might pick up in a charity shop. This was a dress that spoke to Bella.

The rose and crystal clasp sewn on to the neckline was surely a sign. The diamante sparkle of the brooch and pretty satin rose entirely echoed the crystal and rose theme of the three-tiered wedding cake that Bella had triumphantly designed on the fateful day of her sacking.

The dress and the cake could have been made for each other. The cake had been designed for Yvonne's last-minute demand for another programme. The audience had even written in for the recipe. Bella would never have guessed that this particular dress would have the same features as her cake. Let alone be winking at her from across the road when she sat in the window seat in Carmel's Cakery.

Chapter Two

Carmel finally left the kitchen with a plate of scones and a warm freshly baked carrot cake.

'Hello you!' she said to Bella, and proudly placed the cake on a display stand on the counter. Bella moved in for a closer look. She could almost lick the icing from here. This was her absolute, most favourite cake in the land. Surely a happy day lay ahead. A cosy carroty scent enveloped her like spring rain. She decided she could quite happily die from carrot cake inhalation.

If Carmel found it unusual for a customer to be crouched over the counter and smiling at cake, she didn't show it. Instead she and the buttered scones headed over to the lady in the corner with the shopping trolley.

Bella felt her heart sink a little. She hoped they would not start a long conversation. She needed to get Carmel's attention.

'Miserable morning!' Bella called out as the scones were set down. 'Is that a new carrot cake?' she added, to keep Carmel focussed on her.

'Course it is. Up at five I was. Done a coffee 'n' walnut and all. Fancy a slice of each, do you?'

'I'll go for the carrot if I may.' Bella wanted to be very clear. Nothing worse than being given the wrong cake. Although she might try a slice of coffee and walnut before returning for seconds on the carrot.

'You sit down. I'll bring it over when I'm done over here.' Carmel's firm tone suggested Bella should no longer hang around the counter, coughing over the cakes and dripping her wet umbrella everywhere.

Bella stepped back from the counter with a sigh. She couldn't control the timing of her order now and the annoying old lady with the scones might be wanting extras. Or she might take out a wallet of photos of grandchildren to show to Carmel. *All of which would hold up the arrival of cake.*

Bella retreated into her familiar world of make-believe to cope with the fact she had no such family snapshots of her own to show off. Images of Bella with a husband, Bella with a family, Bella the centre of attention at happy family gatherings, played out like a Hollywood film in her mind. Though deep down she knew it was pointless. Forty-year-old women like her didn't get two chances at life and she'd already messed up one. Pregnancy at sixteen had been an accident, but giving up the baby had been deliberate. Her mother had insisted on it. And since then it had just seemed easier to throw herself into the make-believe of daytime television than risk a real relationship. On TV, perfect families appeared on perfect sofas and talked about their perfect lives ...

Bella's attention was caught by a bowl of gingerbread men biscuits on the counter, usually reserved for troublesome children who couldn't wait for a glass of milk or Ribena.

'Can I just take one of these? For now?' Bella raised her voice and shook a biscuit at Carmel.

'Help yourself.'

Carrying the biscuit Bella swiftly plonked her umbrella across the window seat. She tapped it to make sure it left a damp patch to discourage any other users. Then she guiltily wiped the worst off with a napkin.

As the comfort of the tangy dough soothed away her worries, Bella looked again at the bridal shop opposite. She needed to see The Dress. The book *Making Sense of Being Sacked* had indeed 'made sense'. By finding a 'vision of something nice' (even if it wasn't George Clooney) she had helped herself focus on the positive. Fantasies of a crystal-and-rose-themed wedding suddenly took over. There would be crystal and rose nameplates for the women guests and for the men she'd design ... Well the men didn't matter, did they? Men always disappointed in the end. But this dress would never do that. It could never be like a man, or worse, her stupid misguided mother. This was a dress that was a sparkling beacon of hope, of beauty and lasting happiness, and of everything that wasn't horrible. She could even hear herself humming something like the wedding march. It must have been quite loud because she suddenly caught sight of the old lady staring at her. Bella shook herself. She must get a grip.

She took out her glasses and put them on. Then she took out the local paper from her bag and settled down to read. She would do what other people did on their coffee breaks. Maybe there was a crossword puzzle?

Front page first. A youth had been stabbed in a chip shop in the centre of town, but they had already arrested another youth so there wasn't much more to report. Katie Boyle's cousin had opened a dog beauty salon which took up a few more columns than the stabbing. On the opening night one dog had eaten the owner of the shop's handbag but the owner didn't seem to mind, according to the newspaper report.

Bella took a bite of the gingerbread man. She told herself the carrot cake would be with her soon. Carmel had disappeared into the kitchenette. How long did it take to cut a slice and shove it on a saucer?

Bella's gaze wandered back to the bridal shop. A week ago the dress had shared window space with a monster: a 'mother of the bride' dress, in beige, which would have been more suitable for a 'nan of the bride', in support tights and sensible shoes.

But the 'beige' had now been bought (presumably by a nan with no taste) leaving The Dress to twinkle and feed Bella's dreams. The clasp was not too brash and not too flash. Just big enough to sparkle over the white layer of antique lace which fitted neatly round the bodice. From under this cloud of lace dropped the palest cream and pink layered chiffon.

Bella let herself melt further into a fantasy where admiring crowds would all be staring at her in the dress, straining to notice every detail.

Chapter Three

Carmel slammed the carrot cake down on the table. 'Still there then?' she asked Bella.

'I am, yes,' Bella agreed, confused. She hadn't been given her cake yet. Carmel too looked confused for a second. 'The dress. It's still there. The suit's gone, thank goodness. Horrible that was. Muddy parsnip, didn't you say?'

Bella turned her round, streaked face to Carmel's square and sweaty one. She was solemn.

'If I was a mother of the bride I'd shoot myself before I wore a parsnip coat-dress to my daughter's wedding.'

She quickly picked up her fork to cut herself the first chunk of the carrot cake, thinking she'd probably said too much about herself. Too often she lingered on thoughts of the daughter her mother had decided she should give away, wondering what she might be missing.

Carmel caught the note of sadness and hovered by the table.

'My mum wore a borrowed tent dress with

13

flowers on for my wedding. Bit loud but different,' she offered.

'It would be,' agreed Bella.

'What about your mum? What would she go for if you ever …?'

'My mother's not the kind of person you should include in … important events.' Bella tried to limit her 'mother thinking' time to birthdays and Christmas. These events were not the happy occasions that she was sure other, normal, people experienced.

Childhood memories of her mother sprang into focus. She would wait for Bella to get home from school, but only to check who she was walking home with. She'd go through Bella's satchel to see if there were any notes from people who shouldn't be writing notes. Her mother must have been on her side once … maybe. But she couldn't remember when.

'Not that you would tie the knot, would you?' concluded Carmel, filling in the silence. 'Being as you're one of them career ladies.'

'Past tense.'

'You never know what's round the corner, do you though? Coffee?'

'Go on, then.'

Bella forced herself to return to the newspaper rather than wallow in memories. She turned the page to find a large photograph of Yvonne and a group of Bella's ex-colleagues. They were cutting a small cake with the words 'Finger Food' on it, in bright yellow icing.

Bella felt sick. Worse was to come. Below the photograph she read the words 'Flair 4 Living TV launches its new flagship programme in the form of a TV pilot. A low-brow food and chat show called *Finger Food*. Tickets still available. Recording this Friday.'

What was her pilot idea doing in the paper?

Bella must have let out a strange wail of anguish, since Carmel came over to her table. Even the old lady stopped to stare. This scream was louder than the humming.

'You all right, dear?' asked Carmel. 'Went down the wrong way?'

'No. Look. Look.'

Bella was beside herself. She pointed at the page.

Carmel squinted at it. 'I see what you mean. That cake looks a bit squashed and undersized – especially for a party.'

'That's Yvonne. The woman who … let me go.'

'She looks smart.'

'Anyone can look smart in black.'

'Not everyone. Mrs Green, do you think this

15

lady's smart?' Carmel was put out that Bella didn't agree and wanted back-up.

Mrs Green looked pleased to be involved and shuffled over. She appeared to recognise the subject matter.

'It's that TV channel, isn't it. Can't stand it,' she said very definitely.

Bella warmed to her. 'I used to work there. Yvonne's the bossy old cow in black,' she said with feeling. This was lost on Carmel who said mildly, 'Looks well on her, though. Look at that necklace! Bigger than the cake!'

'So she should look well. Yvonne's nicked all my programme ideas and made a fortune. *Finger Food* was my last one. That's my idea of a low-brow …' Bella then read out her own stolen words from the paper, outraged.

'She's even nicked my *description* of the title for the pilot.'

'Which pilot?' asked Carmel.

'Why would a pilot want a title as well? Don't they get paid enough?' Mrs Green added.

'A pilot is a try-out television programme,' explained Bella. 'The one they're doing …' she looked at the paper again. 'God, it's today. Today! They're doing my programme idea today!'

'Yes, we got that.' Mrs Green turned back to Bella. 'Well, it won't be any good, dear. Those presenters should be shot. I saw one silly girl trying to bone a trout and put her lip gloss on at the same time. Making a right hash of both.'

'That was my chance,' said Bella. '*Finger Food* was my chance to try out as a presenter. I'm sure they would have given me the job if they'd seen me.' She slumped at the table.

'Have another little looky at the dress again,' said Carmel kindly. 'Wonder who bought that beige number? Wouldn't it be funny if it was your own mum who bought it and it really was a "nan of the bride's dress", like you said? You got any sisters?'

'No. I'm an only child. Her one great hope,' replied Bella.

'Oh. No pressure then.'

'But ...' Bella felt like talking now. The strain had got to her. 'My mother had the chance to be a ... a ...' she couldn't quite say the word.

'A nan?' offered Carmel, who had seen all types pass through her tea shop and had a very good sense of when they needed to talk and when they didn't.

'Yes, she could have been a "nan". But being sixteen ... it wasn't done. Well she said it wasn't done so I had to ...'

'You had to do what, love?' Carmel asked more intently.

'Give her away,' said Bella quietly, looking at her empty saucer. She turned to look at Carmel, her eyes suddenly blazing.

'And I can't forgive her. I just can't.'

'What about the father?'

'Ian was … perfect, but my mother, she was … so sure at the time and I was so …' Bella trailed off.

'So young,' Carmel finished for her. 'No use looking back, though, Bella. Like I said, you never know what's around the corner.'

Bella had an urgent need to blow her nose.

'You're right,' she said, but didn't sound convinced.

Being out of work was dangerous. At least when she was on the studio floor Bella could block out her sadness with food. Now she had too much time to think about the past.

Bella was just about to order an urgent second helping of cake when her phone rang.

The words 'Flair 4 TV' blazed on her phone strip. Fumbling, she wrenched it from her bag.

'Hello?' said Bella. Maybe Sharon was bored and wanted to chat to someone lower down the pecking order. But to her great surprise it was Yvonne's high hysterical voice which replied.

'Darling, how are you?'

Bella was in shock but mustered enough

sense to lie. 'Busy Yvonne. Pretty busy,' and then before she could stop herself she added, 'Have you had any of the messages I've been leaving for the last six months?'

'Yes, well, that's why I'm ringing. Well, actually it isn't. But can you come in to the studio this afternoon?'

'Why?'

There was a pause. Bella could hear Yvonne take a big breath. Bella hardly dared breathe herself.

'To, er ... to present *Finger Food*. We're doing this pilot called ...'

'I know exactly what the pilot's called. It was my idea,' Bella snapped back.

This was ignored. 'I'll have a car pick you up? Where are you?'

'I'm ... I'm at work.'

'Can I get you another slice of anything?' shouted Carmel in her ear. 'Cappuccino? You've made good work of that carrot cake, haven't you, Bella – that's my girl. You stop wallowing! Nasty boss or no nasty boss!'

Bella pointed at her phone hoping this would make Carmel back off. It didn't. She folded her arms, waiting for another order. It was clear she expected a full reply. Especially as they had shared an intimate exchange only seconds before.

Bella mimed a 'Yes please to both', and nodded furiously.

A silence played out on the phone as Bella wondered how best to respond. If Yvonne was actually offering her the dream job, she couldn't be seen to jump at it. But Yvonne was so reliably mean she couldn't afford to play it too cool, either. She might change her mind just to spite her.

The only thing Bella knew for certain was that she'd never get another chance like this.

'I'll get back home soon,' she said, hoping she was speaking loudly enough to drown out the sound of plates being cleared away.

She would go to the hairdressers, pick up her trousers from the dry cleaners and get her nails done. She'd have to pass on the upper lip wax.

Yvonne interrupted. 'No. Make it half an hour ... you can't be far. I'll send a car to your house.' The phone went dead.

Bella sat stunned for a moment, holding the phone in her hand. No manners. No 'How are you? Hope you don't mind me nicking all your ideas'. Just 'you can't be far. I'll send a car'.

In all her time working for Flair 4 Living TV, dreaming of being a presenter, Bella had never imagined her dream would come true quite so suddenly.

Even as a lowly chopper-upper she had been in her element. Bella was always bounding about the studio, clearing up after second-rate presenters, inventing recipes or pitching one of her themed ideas for programmes. It was Bella who had suggested the Easter picnic hamper prize for guessing the weight of her special three-tiered crystal and rose wedding cake. This had got the viewing figures high for that week. It was Bella who had started the campaign for carnation petals in a savoury salad. That made its way into the *Herald* as 'strangest meal of the week'. Bella was the 'ideas girl' and everyone knew it. Even Yvonne.

So the fact that she was calling her in to present the show could mean only one thing.

Yvonne must be desperate.

Chapter Four

Bella took a deep breath as she took in the familiar studio. She had cleaned and decorated this space for years. She'd seen it dressed in all manner of different guises for various programmes.

But today at the back of the set the words 'Finger Food' twinkled upwards in pink neon flashing lights. This time she was going to … she could barely allow herself to say the word … This time she was going to present a daytime show. Even if it was an experimental pilot, it was still her show. And if Yvonne wouldn't let on that *Finger Food* was Bella's idea she'd just have to put up with it. For now.

She looked again at the studio with the new set design. Two rows of stacked seating had been laid out at one end for the audience. The brightly lit square where the filming took place was defined by black and white squares of lino on the floor … There was brightly coloured kitchen equipment and a counter. She gave a little shudder of excitement.

Bella guessed that behind the counter would

be the usual mess of props rubbish and scripts. She took a quick peek and found she was right. A few apple cores, some electric cable and loads of coconuts. She'd have to be careful not to get tangled up, especially as she might be under pressure. What a leap! From unemployed to under pressure in one hour!

There were three cameras in front of the set arranged to swivel in an instant to capture the audience looking enthralled and happy. If they looked bored or distracted the cameras could swivel swiftly away. She drove back the rising panic in her chest. This was her show. She was going to make it work.

In front of the 'kitchen' area were two sofas in bright yellow-and-pink stripes with shiny cushions in clashing greens and reds.

Bella moved a few cushions and props before lining up the knives neatly and obsessively. She polished off a half empty crisp packet left on the counter to calm her nerves.

The journey to the studio had been rushed to say the least. She'd managed to collect her pinstripe trousers from the dry cleaners only to discover they'd been taken up too short and were also too tight. Her carrot-cake intake during the day had topped five large slices so it was no wonder really.

After hair and make up no one will notice, she reassured herself. Bella was looking forward to all the extras offered to presenters. If she was lucky there might even be time for her to ask wardrobe for something to be ironed, like she'd seen other presenters do. With a bit of make-up Bella felt sure she'd look the part.

There was a sudden clatter of high heels. One of the cameramen said, 'Here comes sunshine,' to Bella under his breath. Bella turned to see Yvonne charging down from the upstairs gallery.

She was wearing a black see-through blouse and black pencil skirt with clickety-click black shiny stilettos. Colour did not feature in Yvonne's wardrobe. Even the bra was black. And as usual she was dressed in the kind of outfit which only pencil-thin people could get away with. She walked briskly up to Bella and blew air around Bella's cheek as a greeting.

'You'd better get changed then,' said Yvonne, grabbing all the cushions that Bella had just moved. She replaced them, tutting loudly, and did the same with the knives. 'We're on in ten.'

'What?' Bella had been determined not to let Yvonne throw her, and here she was, floundering in the first ten seconds. She had nothing to change into. She was wearing her outfit!

'What about make-up?' Bella was horrified. Flair 4 Living TV never let a presenter on screen without make-up. Everyone knew a professionally applied lip line and gloss cheered up the grumpiest of guests.

Bella could see Louise the make-up girl hovering with her bag of tricks at the back of the set.

'What about Louise?' she added, breathing out in relief. 'She can do a five-minute fix.'

But Yvonne was too quick for Bella.

'Sadly Louise has got to do all five presenters of *Master Pet* now, haven't you, Louise?'

Louise looked surprised.

'Haven't you, Louise?' Yvonne's voice dropped dangerously. 'Off you go.'

To Bella's dismay Louise scuttled off.

'Does *Master Pet* have five female presenters?' She smiled at Yvonne brightly in disbelief. 'I thought it was just dogs and that old vet?'

'We've made a lot of changes at Flair since you left.'

'Clearly,' said Bella, forcing a smile. She decided being rude to Yvonne was too much of a risk.

'So! A suit!' Yvonne looked Bella up and down with distaste.

'I know!' said Bella. 'I didn't have time to correct the trousers or get my shoes ...'

'Oh yes. Your corrective shoes!' Yvonne sneered. 'You've got that rather weird thing going on with one your feet, haven't you!'

'Weird? Do you mean my extra toe?' Bella kept her voice casual. This was typical of Yvonne. The toe was an unwanted genetic gift from her mother's side of the family, but she'd ceased to let it bother her long ago. 'I don't need corrective shoes. Those are for people with bunions,' she added, looking at Yvonne's feet.

Yvonne managed a tight half smile and strode away.

'So ...' Bella was determined to make the best of the situation. She rubbed her hands together and looked around at the sudden influx of crew scurrying around the set. Then she hitched down her trousers to release some caught flesh.

'These will work, I think ...' she said to no one in particular. 'A tad snug around the old la la, but that won't show on television ... it's just head and shoulders ... like the newsreaders ... and they wear what they want to underneath, don't they ...? I mean you don't want to know what Moira Stewart used to wear!'

Her favourite cameraman chuckled. A sound man darted forward and asked Bella if she'd mind him fixing a microphone on her. He then felt all over her chest saying 'whoops!' and 'sorry!' as he kept changing his mind about the best way to put his microphone into her blouse.

'You smell nice,' said Bella, because she knew it was good to get on with the crew.

'Thanks. Just had some toast,' he replied.

A girl hurried on to the studio floor with a clipboard. She was wearing a T-shirt with 'Finger Food' written on the front and 'Flair 4 Living TV' on the back. It was tucked into boyfriend-style jeans which were tucked into well-used Ugg boots. The girl was the same height as Bella but slimmer. Her hazel eyes appeared friendly, but her long hair was sticking out at strange angles from her ponytail, in which there was also a pencil. Bella wondered if the pencil was securing the ponytail or had just ended up there by accident. The girl was wearing an earpiece and mouth microphone that bent round her face. It gave her an official manner that the rest of her appearance didn't match. She was too natural-looking and short to be another Yvonne.

She rushed up to Bella with a panicked look.

'Hi hi hi!'

'Hi,' repeated Bella.

'You must be ...' The girl checked her clipboard 'Bella? Hi Hi.' She gripped Bella's hand firmly but looked distracted.

28

'Hi, I'm Fiona?' she said, making the introduction sound like a question. Bella decided she liked her. The girl reminded her of herself when she had just started working at Flair. Slightly overwhelmed but always excited to be here.

'Are you?' said Bella. She was bracing herself for the return of the sound man. He had warned her he might be back with some 'gaffa' tape, whatever that meant.

Fiona looked confused for a second and then decisive. 'Yes, I am.'

Yvonne's voice boomed out from the upstairs gallery. She couldn't be seen but she could certainly be feared.

'Fiona! Tony says he's on his way. Biscuits?'

'Biscuits?' Fiona looked frozen with fear. 'Biscuits,' she repeated as though she hoped this might make them appear.

'Yes, biscuits.'

Bella said, 'I saw some Garibaldis on the sink, there. Will there be real water running from the taps, Yvonne, or are they pretend? Just so I know.'

'Yes, there will be water,' snapped Yvonne. Fiona retrieved the biscuits from the sink and was offering them to no one in particular.

'Fiona! The audience are coming in! Do your stuff. You are the floor manager.'

'Sure yes. I am indeed. Can't wait.' She looked sick with nerves.

As Yvonne clicked her way down the stairs to get at the biscuits Bella moved towards Fiona and whispered, 'She used to be thin and ugly, you know. With braces.'

Fiona's eyes widened in surprise. 'How do you know?'

Bella smiled. 'I've known Yvonne since we were twelve.'

'That long?'

'We were in the Guides.' Bella leaned in closer, relishing the chance to dispel Yvonne's illusion of sophistication. We wore awful uniforms and got badges for lighting fires and knitting blankets. If you got loads you got made a patrol leader. I was made one, but Yvonne never even made second in command. Nobody liked her.'

Fiona stifled a laugh and looked after Yvonne's angry retreating figure.

'Don't say anything but they still don't,' she whispered, adding, 'Braces? Was she very ugly?'

'Mostly. She never smiled. Even when they came off.'

'No difference there, then.' Fiona thought for a moment. 'Is that why she doesn't like you? Because you remember her from before? I heard her talking about you before you arrived.'

Bella felt herself flinch. 'That's part of the reason,' she admitted, regretting having brought it up. The other detail of their shared past was a little more delicate. At Guide camp, Yvonne and Bella had both fallen for the same boy, Ian Smith, in the Scout group. He had been attracted to Yvonne at one point (the day her braces came off, in fact) but ended up going out with Bella. And despite Yvonne's best efforts at sabotage (a dirty-tricks campaign so nasty that Bella could hardly bear to recall it) Bella had enjoyed the happiest summer of her life with Ian. That was, until teenage pregnancy had interrupted matters and the happy couple had been broken up by her mother, and Ian's family moved away.

Despite the tragic ending Yvonne had never forgiven her. Bella could only conclude that this was why she took such delight in giving her the job in the first place. So she could get back at her while making her somehow dependent. She particularly loved showing off her 'special' relationship with Tony who was the boss of Flair 4 Living TV. But, to Yvonne's annoyance, Bella had always preferred to throw herself happily into her work rather than compete for Tony's attentions, whether this was by chopping vegetables or coming up with strange new ideas for programmes to increase the viewing figures.

Annoyingly for Yvonne, these ideas were sometimes not only good, they were also liked by Tony. Which was why Yvonne made sure Bella was never near Tony when he popped in to the studio.

Fiona looked as if she was going to ask something else but then decided not to, instead sharing a secret of her own. She smiled shyly. 'I'm a bit distracted today. I'm in love.'

Taking Bella's silence as a sign of interest, she launched into a high-speed explanation.

'Yeah and he's called Zee Zee. He's from Morocco where it's quite sunny with lots of nice cushions and carpets ... I love his passion and his politics ... and his cute ponytail ... and ... and his customs, like when he gets angry he does what his family does and he throws a shoe at people because that's like the biggest insult over there.'

Bella nodded faintly. Fiona was captivated by her own thoughts of Zee Zee and wouldn't be stopped. Bella was equally captivated by the prospect of presenting a TV show.

'Yeah, like, if you call someone a "shoe" you could be arrested, he said, because it's really rude ... and showing the sole of your shoe is like ... well, it's considered unclean. Mine are always unclean obviously but that's only because I have to walk across the common with all the doggie doo-doos,' continued Fiona raising her foot in demonstration. 'But anyway he threw a shoe at me once. I knew it was my fault because we talked about it afterwards ... and he told me it was ... so it must have been! And he only threw a slipper. And it missed. Just got the goldfish ... who's quite old, so couldn't see it coming ...' She tailed off with a blissful expression. 'So ... you know ... if you see me texting you'll understand!' she concluded, waving her mobile phone.

'I do.' Bella's heart sank. She was about to present a programme but she hadn't even seen a script. The audience were coming in, Yvonne still hated her, Tony the boss was coming ... And now the floor manager who she had to rely on for everything was so lovesick she didn't know if she was coming or going.

Bella felt like screaming. Instead she gripped her fists. She must draw on her experiences of watching all the other bad presenters she'd chopped onions for. After years of watching them she knew how to speak, slice and smile at the same time, only better. It was her big chance to prove herself and she wouldn't let it slip away.

Chapter Five

'OK.' Bella pulled herself together. 'First things first. Can I have the script?'

'Script?'

'The script. Of how the show will run. The running order.'

Fiona looked at her blankly.

'The order of the items? Who comes on, and when, and what I say and which props I'll need for each item.'

'Ah. Yes, I saw one of those.'

'Great. May I have one?'

'But it might not have been for this show.' Fiona saw Bella's look of panic. 'I could ask around?'

Bella had another thought. 'Where's the autocue? I can go through that while you find me the right script.'

'Oh, autocue. Yes. The lady phoned. She's not in today.'

'Right,' Bella was speaking slowly and carefully, 'so I have no script, no autocue. How am I supposed to know what I am presenting?'

Fiona looked unsure. 'Yvonne said you were familiar with *Finger Food*.'

'I am. But I still don't know what's been decided on for today's show.'

'Right. Well, the best thing is ... I'll find you a script, shall I?' said Fiona.

But as she raced away Bella saw her take out her phone, scrutinise the display and then veer off towards a small group of elderly people who had begun to file into the studio with an array of walking sticks and shopping trolleys.

If this was the *Finger Food* audience Bella's hopes of getting whoops of recognition were fading. Getting them to join in could also be a challenge. Fiona seemed to be pushing some of the slower ones quite roughly into seats. Someone should tell her old people are quite frail, thought Bella. There were about twelve of them, including a St John Ambulance lady who had pulled out a large bag of knitting. Yvonne had clearly not gone all-out to draw a lively crowd.

Fiona stepped onto the studio floor and began her 'warm up' of the audience. She held up a few big cards which instructed them to 'applaud!' or to 'go crazy!'

Normally the floor manager would explain to the presenter which shot they were doing first and where they should be. But Fiona seemed to have forgotten. With a sinking heart Bella looked at the phone gripped tightly in Fiona's hand, and realised she was on her own.

She moved to the side of the studio where she'd seen other presenters wait for their introduction.

But then she looked down at the pinstripe trousers and had a sudden crisis of confidence. They really were too snug for a live audience who would see 'everything' when she made her entrance. She caught a sudden glimpse of the wardrobe lady far back in the set, and made a snap decision. There was time, she decided, for a quick change. She whipped the trousers off and called the wardrobe assistant over, waving the trousers in the air.

'Hello … hello there, ladies and gentlemen … this is exciting.' Against all the odds Fiona had got her audience seated and was doing the introduction. Bella swore under her breath. The wardrobe lady had at least understood her request and was going through a rail of clothing. But she wasn't doing it fast enough.

'My name is Fiona, I'm the floor manager … of *Finger Food* … it's my first time actually *managing* a floor so … right, hello and welcome to Flair 4 Living TV. We've got a great show lined up for you today … oh sorry, the lady who's presenting the show today is probably going to say that when she comes on. So act surprised if she does say that, could you?'

Bella tried to signal the wardrobe lady to move faster.

'Oh, and hands up anyone who's in an exciting new relationship? Just me then? Oh well ... but I am committed to my job, I mean I can multitask. And the doors are there if you need them ... oh and please turn your mobiles off ... I'm leaving mine on ... in case I get a call from my lover! And what else ... Oh yes! We've got the owner of Flair 4 Living TV popping in today. He's called Tony, which is why we've got the biscuits.'

Waiting in the wings Bella gave a sigh of relief. Fiona was gabbling in her nervousness. And now the wardrobe lady was headed towards her holding a handful of trousers. *Any* trousers would do. She didn't feel the aging audience were quite ready for her white mottled thighs and big pants.

'Well, let's get the lady on stage. Ladies and gentlemen, I give you Miss Bella Le Parde!'

The *Finger Food* jingly-jangly music took Bella by surprise. She crouched instinctively as the studio lights shone out.

'Dressing gown, DRESSING GOWN!' Bella

was yelling in panic. But the wardrobe lady had disappeared, thinking her job was done. Luckily Louise the make-up girl had come back and thrust a make-up bib in Bella's direction.

'Ladies and gentlemen. Bella Le Parde!' Fiona sounded uncertain now. There was some repeat clapping, slightly quieter this time.

Grabbing a handful of trousers, Bella put on the make-up bib and rushed on stage. It was only when the warmth of the lights hit her bare legs that she realised. She should have put on the trousers, not the bib.

'Hello, ladies and gentlemen.' She tried for a professional tone. 'Err. I'll be coming on again as I've got a slight issue in my trouser department. But I'll just come on now so it's not a shock for people later. Sorry about that but I've just got to make a decision about these.'

Bella held up the trousers.

There was a moment of stunned silence from the audience and then a single old man began to applaud. Fiona rushed on with a tea towel. She held it uncertainly between Bella's midriff and the curious crowd.

'The colour, you mean, Bella?' asked Fiona. 'It is a bit icky. What do you think, ladies and gentlemen?'

The audience began to murmur. Opinion

seemed to be divided but most of them felt a pair of trousers would be an advantage.

'Especially as it's a food programme,' Bella could hear one woman murmuring to her friend. To make matters worse an old man called out cheerfully, 'Like your drawers, love!'

Mortified, Bella walked backwards to crouch behind the counter.

'I'll just pop these ones on if I may. They are woollen but I believe they have been worn by Anna Ford way back, so at least they've got historical interest. Excuse me.'

Bella disappeared behind the counter to put on Anna Ford's old woollen trousers.

From the upstairs gallery Yvonne's voice boomed out, trembling with anger.

'Can we go again, Bella? Fiona, you fill while Bella gets herself decent. Now please.'

A hiss of static revealed that Yvonne had not switched off her microphone button from the gallery. So the whole studio could hear her yell to whoever else was in the gallery with her, 'Unbelievable ...!'

Fiona popped her head over the counter to whisper down to Bella.

'Not sure if you've made the right choice about Anna's trousers, Bella. Wool's not the most forgiving of fabrics. Just being honest!'

'I appreciate that, Fiona, but frankly I'll just have to stick with these. I think I'm ready now,' she added, straightening up with as much dignity as she could muster. 'Do you have the script?' she added in a hiss.

Fiona looked blank, and before she could answer the jingly-jangly music played for the third time and a patter of applause rang out.

Bella took a breath. She felt in a total muddle without a script or decent trousers. The ones she was wearing felt like they'd been knitted with cat hair. She felt them begin to itch around the crotch just as she surfaced from behind the counter.

'Hello, and welcome to *Finger Food*.'

She had no idea what came next. Bella swallowed, remembering Yvonne up in the gallery, willing her to fail.

'I'm Bella Le Parde,' she faltered, 'and I'm going to introduce you to some easy but stylish dishes for women who juggle their lives ... and men who juggle theirs, and also youngsters, juggling and older people perhaps not juggling but who can operate a kettle unsupervised ...'

'Cut!' Yvonne's command echoed round the studio. 'Cut! Bella, we're going to move on to the melon boats.'

Melon boats? Bella tried to remain calm. What were melon boats?

'Yup, Yvonne. I'm right on it!' Determined not to be put off, Bella gave her a rather shaky thumbs-up sign.

'Fiona!' screamed Yvonne. 'Make her do the melon boats NOW. Don't let her do anything else. Fill in while she sets up. DO IT!'

Bella fished about behind the counter to locate any likely-looking ingredients for making a melon boat.

Fiona stepped forward, looking warily at the elderly audience. 'Yes ... well ... a lot of people have noticed a subtle change in me ... It might just be an inner glow ... and I don't know how it's going to affect me because ... I haven't had a job since we met! But we text each other every other hour, which keeps me going, and I expect I'll get my morning text any minute now.'

Fiona looked across at Bella who raised a single finger to indicate she needed one more minute.

Fiona nodded to show she understood and turned back to the audience.

'He's called Zee Zee,' she said, 'from Morocco. Lots of nice cushions in his country.' She licked her lips. 'Funny how love can make you feel quite unwell,' she said faintly, leaning forward on the counter for support. Her eyes sought out Bella.

'Can you do it now, Bella, because frankly I'm feeling a bit sick, is that OK? Yvonne made me eat some of the food colouring earlier to test it and it doesn't seem to be sitting too well.'

'I'm ready,' said Bella, feeling anything but. She quickly removed the food colouring from her box of ingredients. She had found three melons and some cocktail sticks and napkins on the floor under the counter.

'Action!' called Yvonne from the gallery, without waiting for her to get into position. Bella lurched forward with her box, wondering how best to start.

Chapter Six

Sea shanty music blared out, and Bella took the melons out of the box and placed them on the countertop.

'Now, the joy of these little dainties is that everyone can make them,' she found herself saying. She was happy, she realised. She was with food. And if she wasn't sure what kind of food, she could make things up. As the music faded out she got into her stride.

'Let's face it, everyone's got a melon haven't they?' she said, holding one up in explanation. She glanced quickly at Fiona who was smiling encouragingly.

'Everyone's got napkins and everyone's got cocktail sticks and, if they haven't, everyone can go out and buy them because these are the ingredients you'll need.'

Taking the nearest melon, Bella sliced it deftly in half and scooped out a portion. She took a napkin and fashioned it into a sail. The audience watched as the melon was transformed into a table display.

'Looks nothing like a boat, Bella!' Yvonne's voice sounded out, and a slice of melon slipped from Bella's hand.

'And another use of these yummy scrummies is that, er, you could make them into a swimming pool area for a pet budgie if your budgie wanted a water feature which it could also nibble on.'

Bella couldn't see the audience under the bright studio lighting. The old people were attentive, but silent.

Bella started to babble. She started to think up more unlikely uses for her 'melon boats', each of them crazier than the last. Eventually the sea shanty music abruptly started up again loudly, followed by some swearing from the gallery. It seemed no one had dared tell Yvonne that her voice button had been left on and the audience perked up at the fruity language.

'Cut!' Yvonne changed the tone of her voice, in the belief that this was the first the audience was hearing from her.

'Bella, just make the melon boats look as normal as you can. NOW!'

The sea shanty music started again, Bella took a firm hold of the melon and tried to block out thoughts of Yvonne being cross. She put on her best presenter smile.

'So simply hollow out the melon which I've done here, and then put on the sail and very quickly ... don't get worried about knots or other sailing know-how ... I've prepared these sails earlier but you don't have to. You just have to believe and say, I'm a boat, I'm a canoe, let's rock!'

She was enjoying herself, she realised and the audience were laughing along with her. Then she caught sight of Fiona who was madly trying to signal some instructions at her by waving her arms about. After a moment or two it came to her that Fiona was telling her to move the melons so that a camera could do a close-up shot of them.

She tilted the melon boats a little nearer the camera.

A screen flashed an image of how the melon boats should have looked. Totally different to Bella's, but, she thought with pride, not as well put together. The comparison brought a surge of confidence. She'd been thrown onto the set with nothing more than a box of melons and napkins and had made something better than a researcher with hours to dream up a display.

With a little smile of triumph Bella turned to Fiona to try to find out what the next challenge might be. But Fiona had now turned her back on the audience and was whispering into her phone in a worried way. Bella could just hear her.

'I'm saying it's up to you, but if I have, in any way, done something to make you not want me ... do text me. Maybe in the next half-hour ... because then I can truly accept whatever crime I may have committed ... in the name of love ... and I'll learn to never upset you ... ever again. If you're dead or lying run over in a ditch somewhere, then please try to make contact ... use predictive texting to save energy until the ambulance gets there ... bye ... oh it's me, bye.'

'Fiona, could you focus, please!' Yvonne's voice boomed out and everything came to a halt. 'Unless you want to be sacked immediately. Bella! Move to the sofa area! Introduce the first guest.'

Then while Yvonne thought no one could hear she muttered, 'They're as bad as each other. Unbelievable.'

While the set was in chaos the audience had perked up no end. The old man who had liked Bella's 'drawers' turned to the St John Ambulance lady with the knitting. 'This beats *Emmerdale* hands down!' he announced.

Bella headed towards the brightly coloured

sofas to do an interview with someone. She had no idea who this might be. Then she caught sight of Fiona pointing. Following the direction of her finger she saw that a dog-eared handwritten note lay on the sofa.

Bella grabbed it and saw to her relief that it contained a few facts about the guest. She squinted at the writing. Fiona had jotted down some details, but it was a scribble of mad text rather than clear points.

Cora Johnson, she mouthed to herself, trying to memorise the information. Meals on Wheels.

Without warning another jingle blared and the cameras swung in on Bella.

In a voice she hardly recognised as her own Bella read in a loud bright voice, 'So now let us welcome our *Finger Food*'s guest of the week on to the pilot ... she has become famous in a matter of weeks ... from a humble Meals on Wheels volunteer to an internationally top-selling cookery writer and campaigner for ...'

She glanced quickly down at the paper.

'Mood-swing food! If you please! What's that about? Let's find out. Please welcome Mrs Cora Johnson!'

Chapter Seven

A large woman of middle years in a tweed suit almost ran on to the set in a state of great excitement. She stood twitching slightly. Bella stared meaningfully at the luminous yellow sofa.

The sound of Yvonne's muttering echoed through the studio.

'Sit, sit, you big dod of lard.'

Clearly no one was going to risk telling Yvonne her radio mike was broadcasting every remark to the wider floor. Cora was too excited to consider this remark could be about herself and remained standing and smiling. Bella stood up and guided her firmly to a seat on the sofa.

'Hello, Cora, and welcome!'

Cora leaned forward. Bella hoped this would be a quick interview and over soon.

'Well, Cora, being a lowly Meals on Wheels volunteer you must be thrilled with your sudden fame …'

Cora started babbling. 'Yes, I am … yes. I'm being let off work to do the publicity so it's all very exciting ... I'm heavily pencilled in for *The One Show* next week.'

Bella glanced back at her page and then noticed that Cora had arrived with a recipe book with Cora Johnson across the front.

'So what gave you the idea to write a cookbook with a sausage on the front? I see you've got it there with you.'

'I have!' Cora held up the book delightedly. 'Well, it's a very funny story actually.'

'Fingers crossed!' interjected Bella. The audience laughed.

'I was just doing my normal rounds,' said Cora. 'I cover about twenty miles this side of the M25 and my colleague, Muriel, she covers the north side ... which can take over an hour depending on the traffic ... although I will veer off onto a B road if there's an emergency ...'

'And moving to the snappy and interesting bit?' urged Bella.

The audience laughed again but Cora could not be stopped.

'Well, on a Tuesday, Wednesday and Sunday, we always do a meat and rice dish whereas on a Friday we'll do a fillet of fish with peas ... weekdays can vary, but in the main we offer them mince but anyway, it was always on a Friday I had problems with my gentlemen clients ...'

'She's a volunteer you see, a carer who some people might find quite interesting,' said Bella in a bid to win back the audience. 'Or not,' she added.

The old man who had been chatting up the St John Ambulance lady piped up.

'Not!'

More laughter followed.

'In fact it was only when my neighbour's son came home in an angry mood. Then I made the connection ...!'

Bella felt she saw light at the end of the tunnel. Cora had paused for effect, holding her book aloft.

'Which was?' prompted Bella.

'That certain recipes affect moods. Fish and peas make you angry!'

'Which might explain why Captain Birdseye had such a red face?' offered Bella.

Cora ignored this.

'Whereas rice, pork and peas make you a bit *saucy*. I had to stop wearing skirts on a Friday after that ... it was fairer to the old people really ... even if they had to eat with their fingers. I couldn't risk bending over to pick up cutlery.'

Bella was trying hard to follow. 'And the funny bit of your story?' she ventured.

Cora looked put out. 'It was more funny peculiar.'

'Right.' Bella tried to look interested. 'And your point about the cookbook?'

'Well ...' Cora took a deep breath. Bella winked at the audience and added, 'In your own time', which got a laugh.

'My menus can serve as both a caution and a delight. I mean, what could be better than tucking into one of my creamy pasta dishes at the same time as being warned about a dangerous urge brought on by pork, rice and peas? It's all in the mix, you see.'

Bella nodded, smiled, and moved to wrap things up, hoping that she would never see Cora again. Ever. She looked up at the gallery, silently cursing Yvonne for allowing this terrible guest loose on the show without warning her.

'Well, ladies and gentlemen, there you have it.' Bella turned back to the audience and felt an apology might be justified. Instead she said, 'A stunning array of recipes to put us in a better mood! Do we have any questions?'

The man next to the St John Ambulance lady put his hand up.

'Yes, you, with the bow tie,' said Bella, suddenly feeling in charge. A cameraman swiftly turned his camera upon the man in the bow tie.

Jumping away from her phone Fiona raced towards the audience with a microphone.

'Do you want to come over and see to my sausage, Cora?'

Encouraged by the audience's laughter the man added a rather lewd gesture involving his forearm and a fist. The cameraman had swung away just in time.

Up in the gallery Bella heard Yvonne's muttered swearing. As did everyone else. The audience clearly thought it was part of this rather rude new food pilot.

'Well I think you've made a great hit there, Cora!' Bella stood to lead the guest out. 'Cora! Ladies and gentlemen.'

The audience clapped but Cora didn't budge from the sofa. After an uncomfortable moment Fiona darted in and dragged Cora off. She waved as she went.

Suddenly a man with white hair and a turtle-neck jumper stepped though the side doors of the studio. He'd been watching for a while and was now clapping Cora and Bella.

Bella recognised him instantly. It was Tony, the head of Flair 4 Living TV. She managed to keep the professional smile glued to her face.

Over the turtle-neck he wore a blazer with gold buttons, above check trousers and very pointy leather shoes. He reminded Bella of a cross between Richard Madeley and Basil Brush. Tony waved in a royal way at the audience and said to Bella, 'Carry on!' with a little wink. He put his tongue inside his cheek at the same time and sauntered up to the gallery.

There was an audible gush from Yvonne as he arrived in the gallery. 'Tony? Darling!'

Fiona had returned to the set and looked scared. 'The biscuits are in the gallery,' she said, looking anxiously at where Tony had sauntered off.

There was a pause around the set as the crew waited for Tony to settle himself.

Fiona swivelled over to Bella and said under her breath, 'That was Tony!'

'I know,' Bella replied. She didn't like to see Fiona so frightened.

'He's the boss,' explained Fiona in awe.

'Not quite,' said Bella, deciding to dispel some of the terror Tony put in Fiona. 'His *wife*'s the boss.'

Fiona looked shocked. 'His wife?'

Bella nodded. 'Tony's wife pays for all of this. For your lovely T-shirt, for the studio, for the melons … and, well everything. Without Tony's wife there'd be no Flair 4 Living TV!'

'Imagine!' said Fiona in disbelief.

'Exactly! So how are things with Zee Zee? Any news?' Bella felt a flash of anger. Fiona seemed such a sweet girl. Zee Zee shouldn't be messing her around.

'Well ...' Fiona was about to launch into her favourite subject when muffled kissing sounds came over the gallery. Then the sound of Yvonne's voice.

'I'm so sorry about Bella, Tony ... she's obviously over-excited and panicking. I *told* you she's hopeless and now you can see she is! But worry not! She's only here for ...'

Bella bit back her annoyance.

There were more smooching sounds.

'I thought she was quite good,' said Tony. 'She handled that randy old gent rather well.'

The whole audience turned to look at the man in the bow tie who looked most put out. He stood to his full height of five foot three. 'Old? I'm not old!'

'Is she here?' It was Yvonne again, this time in 'studio mode'.

'Yes. I'm here,' said Bella, looking around in confusion. To her surprise Fiona had gone completely red.

'Yes, we know *you* are, Bella,' said Yvonne. Adding under her breath, 'More's the pity,' and then more loudly, 'I was talking to Fiona. Is she here yet? I was told she would be arriving on the 5.45. Now we've got Tony, I was hoping this ridiculous situation would be resolved.'

'Er ...' Was it Bella's imagination or was Fiona looking in her direction with a very guilty expression. 'Er, yes?'

She must still be upset about Zee Zee, Bella decided. But the fact that Tony was here meant she could finally prove herself as a presenter who had a way with an audience. And even though the first two features had been disasters, she was beginning to enjoy herself.

'Can you get her in make-up then? Bella, can you fill in?'

Bella was again confused. Had Yvonne finally decided that her shining face could do with some make-up, after all? Or should she fill in?

'Who or what do you mean, Yvonne? Make-up or fill in?'

'You fill in.'

Chapter Eight

For once Yvonne wasn't getting to Bella. She was having too much of a good time. She was finally getting the chance to shine. She looked out at the small crowd and stepped forward.

'I'll fill in for a few minutes, Yvonne, no problem. Could we have the healing music on, the CD you use for *Master Pet*?'

'What?' Yvonne sounded anxious. She doesn't want me presenting in front of Tony, Bella realised. She's terrified he'll think I have talent.

'I'm taking the audience into a visual exercise,' explained Bella. 'So if you could just roll the tape, Yvonne.'

There was a loud grumpy sigh followed by a click.

Whale music began to filter out into the studio.

'So if we could all shut our eyes,' said Bella, sliding into a calm version of her presenter's voice. 'That means you as well, Yvonne, thank you.'

Bella glanced out into the audience. They were sitting obediently with their eyes closed.

'Imagine you are on a beach,' she intoned. She noticed Fiona, her eyes wide open, staring at her phone and willing it to ring.

'Are you shutting your eyes, Fiona? Because this really only works if you shut your eyes, and it could very possibly change your life.'

Fiona closed her eyes.

'Can I open them if I get a text?'

'No. It'll be a lovely surprise afterwards ... So imagine you are on a beach or alternatively you can pick a grassy knoll.'

Fiona interrupted again. 'Just to ... er ... clarify, what is a knoll?'

'A knoll is a small hillock,' said Bella, keeping the same calm voice. 'So choose now, or go back to the beach. The waves are lapping for the beach group, and there is a soft mossy carpet of green for the hillock group.'

'I'm on the hillock.' Fiona's face was screwed up in concentration.

'Good, that's reassuring ... now let's send out loving rays. Are you receiving the rays?'

The music cut out suddenly.

'Bella, we've got a hold-up in make-up,' bellowed Yvonne's crisp, mean voice. 'They're sending out for some more hair tongs. Go to the table display quickly, please.'

'Table display,' repeated Bella. 'Table display, Fiona?'

She looked across at Fiona who had sunk down in a chair and was deep in a trance, as were most of the audience. The St John Ambulance lady's knitting had unravelled and her knees had flopped over into the lap of the man with the bow tie.

Bella shook Fiona gently awake, feeling surprisingly maternal. Fiona sprang back into reality and looked around at the studio in confusion.

'Table display?' said Bella. Fiona blinked for a long moment, mouthing the words, and then jumped up and ran off.

Bella went round and clapped the audience awake. They all stretched, had a good yawn and seemed to be in much better spirits than before. The bow-tie man helped the St John lady rewind her wool. Bella thought they made a nice pair and found herself hoping Zee Zee would come through for Fiona. Such a sweet girl.

'Bella!' shouted Yvonne. 'We're running the hairy fruit feature. You should know this one at least.' Then thinking herself off-mike she added to Tony. 'This is some strange little idea Bella came up with after I'd put together the pitch for *Finger Food*, and I thought it was only fair to let her try it out.'

Bella was outraged. She remembered Yvonne suggesting she should add a strange section on making a table display by gluing fruits together. She'd privately thought it would never work but hadn't dared question Yvonne at the time. Now she'd been left to exhibit Yvonne's bad idea and get the blame when it went wrong.

Bella sat herself at the table display area and checked the props list as subtly as she could manage.

Yvonne called, 'Action!'

Imagine yourself to be Nigella Lawson, only with a tube of glue, she told herself.

'So!' She spoke confidently into the camera. 'Let's make a table display with some glue and some fruits. I'm using these pawpaws!' she looked around for the fruit. Fiona rushed on with some coconuts.

Bella said, 'Those aren't pawpaws.'

'I think they're called coconuts, Bella.'

'It says here pawpaws.'

'Which I Googled and it said "hairy fruit" in brackets,' replied Fiona. 'I think. Anyway, I brought some waxing strips as well,' she added helpfully.

Bella decided to change tack.

'Right, ladies and gentlemen. I'm giving these coconuts a Brazilian because I know some people are squeamish about hair ... which is all very *Sex in the City* and should please the chief executive of Flair TV who is busy making decisions about the future direction of the show ... Hi, Tony, if you can see me!' Bella gave a little wink up to Tony.

She then pressed the waxing strip to the coconut and whipped it away with a flourish. She glued the 'de-fuzzed' coconut into a table-display setting with a candle on a saucer and sat back to admire her handiwork.

'Lovely for a family lunch or even a christening,' she declared triumphantly. Confidence was all. There was even a small outbreak of applause.

Yvonne's voice boomed out.

'Bella ... the wine guest has cancelled. Double-booked herself for a tasting.'

'Lucky her!' Bella winked at the audience. 'If only we all had that problem!' But confusion was setting in. Hadn't Yvonne been talking about the arrival of a guest in make-up? Fiona had returned to the floor and was looking distinctly uneasy.

'Fiona, can you ask Bella if she will double as the wine guest?'

Bella looked curiously up at the gallery. 'What? Interview myself, you mean? Won't that look a bit ... er, mad?'

But it seemed Yvonne was no longer talking to Bella.

'Fiona, have you had that *little word* with Bella I asked you to have?'

'What word?' asked Bella, wondering what was going on. 'What "word", Fiona?'

Fiona's face had crumpled and she was staring at the floor.

'I'm sorry, Bella,' she whispered. 'I couldn't tell you. I just couldn't ...'

Yvonne's voice boomed out. 'Fiona, could you tell Bella what we discussed now or you are sacked from this moment forth!'

Bella looked at Fiona kindly.

'You can tell me Fiona? What is it?'

'Look, I can't soften the blow ... err ... Juliet Parker's here so ...'

'Juliet Parker's the next guest? ... But that's fantastic news!'

'Yes, I suppose it is.' Fiona chewed her fingernail. 'She was delayed in Paris at the Ideal Pelmet road show ...'

Bella asked Fiona, 'Am I doing it, then?'

Fiona looked shifty. 'Doing?'

'Doing the interview with Juliet Parker?'

A possible answer as to why Fiona was acting so oddly came to her. She probably thought Bella might fall apart in the presence of such a big celebrity. Juliet had been a top designer on daytime TV in the nineties.

'Fiona, there's no need to worry!' said Bella. 'I'm a huge fan of Juliet Parker. I'm excited, not nervous!'

Fiona was still looking very guilty indeed. But Bella was too excited about doing an interview with her heroine to worry. Juliet Parker was a legend in the daytime TV world of re-designing homes on a budget.

Though Juliet usually hosted shows, so it was a bit strange that she was coming on as a guest ... But Bella was a professional. Well, she was now.

'I can hardly breathe! The scoop of the century! Juliet Parker on my pilot! Can we have the next props then, Fiona?'

But Fiona was back on the phone.

'Zee Zee? I'm just phoning to say that you are everything to me, no pressure or anything ... I'm just leaving a second message now because I realised you might need two, before you reply ... as some sort of test. Also ... if your phone's been robbed and you're the robber listening to this ... could you let me know that he's safe? And that you haven't maimed him too badly? His wallet's in his blazer pocket … help yourself to the Boots' vouchers but leave the photo of us horsing around.'

Bella moved her attention to the audience to keep them as excited as she was.

'Ladies and gentlemen, it gives me great pleasure to introduce someone who is as famous for designing gorgeous sitting rooms as she is for wearing her tight white jeans! And not only that, she is going to help us taste our very own *Finger Food* summer wine selection!'

Bella moved back into the kitchen area to see that a tray of opened wine bottles had been laid out with two glasses. She poured herself a glass and raised it in a toast.

'Ready for Juliet! Cue music!' Yvonne's voice cut across the studio.

Bella took a nervous sip. Then it hit her. She was on TV, interviewing Juliet Parker! Surely this called for a celebration drink! The audience were on her side, she knew they were. She took another few gulps of wine.

'Ladies and gentlemen, I give you Juliet Parker!'

Chapter Nine

With the *Finger Food* jingle playing, Juliet Parker made her entrance. All in white. White tight jeans were teamed with a white kaftan top. Her hair was white (with yellow streaks) and her skin pale (white).

As the wine hit her Bella had a sudden vision of Yvonne and Juliet as black and white queens.

Juliet's trousers were also tight but, Bella noticed, hung fashionably from her slim frame. She looked at her own itchy woollen trousers, courtesy of Anna Ford, with regret. Then Juliet swept past her. 'Hello, hello everyone! At last! I've been stuck on Eurostar first class while they sent someone back to Paris to get me another coffee. Juliet swung round to Fiona. 'I'm dying for a decaf now – I'm all jittery! You couldn't fetch us a coffee, could you sweetheart?'

But Fiona had gone a peculiar shade of green. 'I … I don't feel so well,' she managed, looking pleadingly at Bella. 'All this excitement with Zee Zee. And that food colouring from this morning. I think … I think I'm going to be sick.'

'Go and have a lie down,' whispered Bella. 'We can manage without you.'

She looked at the empty kitchen area. How would the set-up for the final feature get arranged without Fiona? But the poor girl really did look unwell. Bella glanced again at her sweating face.

'Fiona!' Yvonne's voice pierced the studio. 'You're behind with the raspberry ice cream feature. Get the blender and the cakes on set now!'

'But I ...'

'Now! Fiona. Unless you want to be out of a job.'

Fiona scuttled away looking very ill.

Juliet waved up towards the gallery.

'Hello, Yvonne, up there in your box ... Hello Tony, hello darling! I'm wearing the necklace.' She pointed to an expensive-looking diamond at her throat.

'OK Tony, where do you want me?'

Bella opened her mouth and shut it again. Juliet was obviously so used to playing the host that she made a poor guest. Bella would need to take a firmer hand.

'Welcome, Juliet.' She stepped in to guide her towards the wine selection. 'If you could come on here.'

Juliet looked confused.

Bella turned to face the audience and said, 'She's just come from Paris to London in one day, ladies and gentleman! You must be exhausted.'

Juliet smiled with grace. 'Not as bad as last week. I did Milan, New York and Madrid in one day! Shall we do the wine section now, then? Is the guest not here?'

Bella paused for a moment. Juliet must be muddled over how many guests would be appearing.

'Well you're here now!' said Bella cheerfully. Fiona had clearly not managed to brief Juliet properly, but she could cover for the mistake.

'So shall we get on with it?' continued Bella, steering Juliet towards the counter.

Bella poured two glasses of wine and drank a gulp out of both of them. Perhaps she had peaked? She moved back to her seat in a bid to appear more in control.

'I'm starting in five, Juliet, so just to be aware ...' She saw a flutter of paper in Juliet's hand. Why had Juliet been given a script when she, the presenter, hadn't?

'Oh! Are you going to pretend to be my guest?' asked Juliet. 'They told me there was a double-booking with a wine tasting.'

The words floated over Bella as she counted herself in with increased confidence. She took another swig of wine. 'In three, I'll cue myself, we're rolling ...'

As the *Finger Food* jingle began playing Juliet leaned across. 'I love your trousers by the way. Whoever said tight wool can flatter was right.'

The jingle ended and to Bella's annoyance Juliet stood as though she were the host and Bella the guest. This was taking things too far. Bella didn't want Tony to think she was a pushover as a host. She wasn't going to lose her grip now. Even if Juliet was turning out to be a bit of a control freak. Luckily the wine had given her confidence.

'Ooh Juliet!' she said, taking her arm with a little more force than was needed. 'Let's focus! Talk me through the wine ... Being a female designer yourself, you would probably know what kind of labels women are looking for. Wouldn't you?'

Juliet stared at Bella and paused for a second. 'Actually,' she said, in a careful slow voice, 'why don't you take us through the wines since you're still here and raring to go!'

Bella looked at Juliet, wondering whether the wine was affecting her more than she realised. Why was Juliet speaking to her as if she was an idiot?

There were another few seconds of silence.

'So!' they both said at exactly the same time.

'Oh jinx!' said Bella. 'Make a wish! What shall we wish for? I wish I was the highly paid face of Highland Spring facial mist ... oh, but you are! How does she do it, ladies and gentlemen ... seriously, how do you do it?'

Bella felt the audience on her side as they all murmured that they really didn't know. Juliet replied with false modesty.

'It's been busy season since I left the rainforest.'

'Busy for some!' said Bella.

'I'm just lucky,' Juliet flashed back. She flung a tight white denim trouser leg over the other in annoyance, revealing a diamond ankle bracelet that matched the chain around her neck.

'You are not wrong, Juliet,' Bella said. 'She is like a rash, ladies and gentleman! She gets on everything!'

Juliet raised her voice 'I only ever endorse what I've personally used, sat on or tasted.'

The two women glared at each other, waiting to see who would make the next move.

Through the slight fogginess of the wine something was slowly dawning on Bella. The script in Juliet's hand. Fiona's shiftiness. And, above all, the idea that Yvonne, of all people, would give Bella a chance to be a presenter.

It suddenly came to her. Yvonne had cast Juliet to be the presenter. Bella had only ever been a stand-in. And now Bella was expected to stand in as a guest for the woman who had her job. On her show. From *her* idea.

Fiona stumbled onto the set carrying the blender and waving her phone with a free hand.

'I got a text!' she shouted. 'I got a text!' Then she leaned forward and was sick in the blender.

Juliet and Bella, in deadlock, failed to notice. Fiona placed the blender carefully on the counter next to the other cake ingredients.

'What did the text say?' asked Bella, keeping her eyes locked on Juliet.

'Nothing!' Fiona wailed. 'My first blank text! He may be in danger. I'm sorry Bella,' she added. 'I know you should be presenting this show. Yvonne wanted me to tell you about Juliet but I couldn't do it.'

The penny also dropped for Juliet.

She leaned close to Bella, her voice low and threatening.

'Listen, love, I'm working with Claire Sweeney in half an hour ... I've just stepped off a train from Paris ... I've won awards ... do you really think you could host a show like this? Do

72

you really think Tony Trimble would employ you to front-up anything? You are living in a dream world, my lovely …'

Something snapped in Bella. Her mother, Yvonne, and now this white-clad product placement queen telling her what she wasn't capable of.

Bella rose shakily from her wine stool. 'I may be living in a dream world,' she said, her voice raised to the same level as Juliet's. 'But you're not going to take it away from me.'

She picked up a cake knife.

Juliet's eyes widened in horror and the audience let out a howl. The St John Ambulance woman stood up, but the man in the bow tie told her to sit down again. He was having the time of his life.

Bella wielded the knife menacingly.

'Juliet, you're going to help me now in my stunning daytime TV debut. I'll be the toast of *Take a Break*, and housewives up and down the land will pause mid-Dyson to note my handy tips.'

Bella scanned the kitchen area and her eyes settled on a row of cakes laid out with a blender and raspberries for the final feature.

'We're going to make a raspberry ice cream, Juliet,' she said, waving the knife wildly, 'simple,

73

yet brilliant. To be eaten with any other pudding you can think of. And I'll be using real raspberries. Have you ever heard of anything real? *Finger Food* will be like daytime TV should have been, with real personalities.'

She took a step closer to Juliet. 'Go on. Force those raspberries through the sieve.'

Juliet start to whimper but it seemed none of the audience wanted to help her. Some had taken up a chant: 'Go Bella! Go Bella!'

Bella turned to the blender. It was already full of pinkish liquid, which was confusing since the ice cream mix had not yet been made. There was a strange smell to it, too. Not like raspberries at all. She wrinkled her nose.

'You can stop with the raspberries now, Juliet,' she said brightly. Juliet looked nervously at the knife.

'Taste this ice cream,' said Bella. 'Go on, Juliet. Have a taste.'

Juliet recoiled from the blender, which even Bella had to concede did not look much like any ice cream she'd made before.

There was a familiar clickety-clicking as Yvonne's high heels arrived on set.

'Bella!' she shouted. 'I will personally see to it that you never work in television again!'

Fiona grabbed the set of boards which she

used to tell the audience what to do and chose the one which said 'go crazy!' She shook it at the audience and they immediately started clapping in a crazy way. But this only encouraged Bella to shout over the applause.

'I am the voice of the little people,' she shouted, waving the knife at the audience. 'I am the voice of low-brow television. And no, I didn't get left behind, it's the formats that got smaller. When I click my fingers. I, Bella Le Parde, will shape the dreams of those who desire a second bathroom with a budget beach hut feel ...'

Yvonne screamed up to the gallery, 'KILL THE LIGHTS!'

The set was thrown into darkness. Everyone was quiet.

Yvonne yelled, 'PUT THEM ON AGAIN!'

Bella suddenly felt a little dizzy.

Yvonne cleared her throat and addressed the audience.

'I have an announcement to make. I'm sorry, ladies and gentlemen. As you can see we have a very unusual situation. Bella Le Parde will no longer have a place on Flair 4 Living.'

Chapter Ten

To Yvonne's surprise the audience started to boo.

'And Fiona will be sacked for being sick in a TV kitchen implement!' she added.

Bella looked at the blender in surprise.

There were more boos. For a moment Yvonne looked alarmed, but then turned the full force of her fury on Bella, and spoke in a hiss.

'You may have lost me this pilot, Bella, and if you have I will personally see to it that your life is ruined. Now I have to go back and try and persuade Tony Trimble to give this show another chance.'

She turned and retreated upstairs.

There was a pause. Juliet eyed the knife in Bella's hand, as if deciding whether it might be safe to make a run for it.

From the gallery came the sound of Yvonne speaking in a little-girl voice which Bella had never heard before.

'Tony, darling, once we get rid of Bella we

can nail the audience figures! It's a fantastic idea of mine! You said so yourself.'

'The audience seem to be finding Bella rather ... engaging,' replied Tony.

'Oh darling!' smooched Yvonne, 'you're so sweet when you're puzzled. Come here. Come closer.'

'Just for a quickie then. My wife promised to check in on the show.'

A ripple of shock ran through the audience.

'Better than *Emmerdale*,' repeated the old man happily.

There was a sudden scream.

'Noooooooo!' It was Fiona. She had just made sense of what Yvonne had said about her.

'I need my job!' she raged. 'Zee Zee and I are saving for our wedding. I can't be sacked!'

She swept the cakes off the counter and threw two wine bottles across the set. They smashed against the neon 'Finger Food' sign.

'Nooooo!' she yelled again, tearing apart the box of melon rubbish.

Bella ran to calm her down. But before she could get to her Fiona had dropped the box and was tearing off her shoes.

'I'll show them, Zee Zee!' she screamed, aiming a shoe at the gallery. 'If it's an insult for you, it's an insult for me!'

By this time Juliet had also understood what was going on up in the gallery. 'Tony, how could you!' she asked in disbelief. She then decided that a fit of hysteria might be the best way to get attention. Trapped between Bella and Fiona, the strain was too much. She began wailing at the top of her voice.

In an instant, the St John Ambulance lady was on set, pushing Juliet onto the sofa and soothing her.

Normally Bella would have been interested to see the queen of daytime television reduced to wailing. But the moment Fiona had taken her shoes off, all Bella's attention was on her feet.

She pointed at Fiona's toes.

'Fiona! Fiona, your toe.'

'What about it?' Fiona asked, pausing mid shoe-throw, and wiggling her sixth toe.

'I have one of those as well,' said Bella. 'I have six toes too! It runs in the family,' she added, 'on the mother's side.'

Fiona shrugged. 'I never knew my mother,' she said. 'I was given up for adoption as a baby. The papers said my mother was a Girl Guide who was forced to give me up because of her pushy mother. I've only just tracked down my real father 'cos Zee Zee said I had to, and he said that was all true. Oh ...'

She slowly looked at Bella. Bella's mouth fell open. Could it? Could it be?' Your father,' she said very quietly, 'what is his name?'

'Ian,' said Fiona, equally quietly, 'Ian Smith. I wanted to find my real parents because of the wedding. But I only found one of them.'

'Fiona!' Bella could hardly breathe. 'It was me! I was the Girl Guide! I was the one who gave you up. And I've wished every day since ...' The words began to choke her. 'Every day since, that I'd kept you.'

Fiona gasped. Bella threw off her shoes and waved her six-toed foot at Fiona who waved hers back. The audience went wild.

Bella ran to Fiona and they embraced.

There was a party atmosphere on set. The camera was rolling and it looked like a very happy TV show. Fiona's phone went and this time it really was Zee Zee. She gave him a long excited run-down of the events of the morning, leading to discovering her long-lost mother.

When she came off the phone she took Bella's hand.

'Zee Zee's looking forward to meeting you!' she said. 'He doesn't care that I'm out of a job and we can't afford to get married.'

Bella beamed back at her. She had found the daughter she'd always dreamed of. And, somehow, her dream of being a presenter seemed less important. TV could wait, she decided. She would introduce Fiona to Carmel's tea shop and they would catch up on all the years they had lost. She might try to reserve the window seat in advance.

Of course, there was just a tiny tinge of sadness, and who wouldn't be just a bit sad? Her career as a food presenter was over before it had started. But more importantly she felt sorry for Fiona. It was Bella's fault she was out of a job.

The soothing had calmed Juliet down. Now she was no longer wailing, Yvonne and Tony could be heard talking in the gallery.

'My wife will pull the plug on everything if we can't justify the money spent on *Finger Food*,' said Tony.

Bella looked at the cameras. They had been rolling the entire time. She walked to the nearest one and asked the cameraman to give her the tape. He did so with pleasure. Everything Yvonne and Tony had said was on record. Even the things that Yvonne thought no one else could hear.

Bella cleared her throat.

'Could I have silence please?' She called up to the gallery, 'Yvonne! Here's an idea that might help you out of your tangled web. No one thought to tell you that your microphone has been on for this entire pilot. And down here on set we've all been able to hear everything. Everything.' Bella paused to let the words sink in.

'If you give me back MY pilot as a series,' she continued, 'with Fiona as floor manager, I will agree not to tell Tony's wife that Tony, you and Juliet are in a little trio. If you get me.' She waved the tape. 'It's all been recorded.'

'Tony? You and *Juliet*?' Yvonne spoke for the first time.

Tony sounded guilty. 'It was only the once, Yvonne. Nothing happened.'

'So.' Bella decided to make an offer to Tony. 'Since Yvonne seems to be speechless I'll make you an offer you can't refuse. I present *Finger Food*, which is my idea in any case, and Fiona keeps her job.'

Tony emerged on the gallery balcony, straightening his clothing. He looked at the audience and then at Bella.

'Bella, I thought you were magnificent,' he said. 'The audience loved it. I think the show could really work with you at the helm. And,' he winked at Fiona and did that funny thing with his tongue in the cheek again, 'the pair of you as a double act work perfectly.' He blew a kiss.

Bella waved her hand dismissively.

'Oh, keep your kisses for Yvonne. She's such a trustworthy, open-hearted, kind, warm person how could anyone resist?'

The audience booed loudly.

Tony smiled. 'It's a deal.'

Chapter Eleven

The church organist was playing a Middle Eastern melody with some difficulty. Three Moroccan folk dancers joined in as best they could with flutes and drums.

Under the hypnotic effect of the music the guests were swaying as if in a trance. Roses and crystals decorated every seat and a handsome young man was waiting anxiously by the altar.

Bella sat at the front, proudly awaiting the bride. She was wearing a rose-print dress with little crystals on the collar. Next to her sat Carmel in a cream suit and, on her other side, sat Bella's own mother, clutching a lace hankie in readiness. Once Fiona had been found, her grandmother had admitted that she too had always regretted the decision to give her away. She had carried her guilt all through Bella's career but had never once spoken of it. Their relationship had still not recovered – that would be perhaps too much to ask – but Bella's mother was thankful that her daughter had been generous enough to include her in the special day.

As the music changed pace they turned to see Fiona enter the modern, slightly wacky, church. She made her way up the aisle, which had been decorated with crystal roses and Moroccan carpets and bottles of musk oil. The latter were wedding gifts from Zee Zee's family.

All faces strained to get a look at The Dress.

Bella wiped away a tear. Here at last was her dream dress. No longer a dream, and worn by the most special person in her life.

At Fiona's side was a man she recognised. It couldn't be, but it was. Those hazel eyes and shy smile … Yes! Her boyfriend of all those years ago was walking his daughter down the aisle.

Fiona had said there might be the odd surprise, but Bella thought it was just the unusual drumming. She had prepared herself by bringing the earplugs she used for long coach journeys.

Bella looked again. He had hardly changed. A slightly stockier version and not bad-looking at all. Bella assumed he must have a lovely wife and family somewhere and felt a stab of regret. Perhaps he had other children. Perhaps there would be a step-family to meet. Bella drove away these thoughts. Instead she focussed on The Dress. It perfectly reflected Fiona's beautiful gleaming skin and bright hazel eyes. The rose and the crystals shone in the sunlight of the church. The antique lace fluttered, the chiffon sparkled and everything looked as it was supposed to do. It was surely a moment to savour.

The vicar had already proved himself a modern kind of vicar with a sense of humour. As Fiona reached for her husband-to-be's hand, Bella's mother and Bella held each other's hands to brace themselves for more bad jokes.

'It seems this young couple have a lot to be thankful for,' said the vicar. 'Not only is our bride a wonder at whipping up an audience, but her mother is just as good at whipping up a de-fuzzed coconut. A photo of which takes pride of place next to the collection box. Hint hint. Welcome to the entire audience of *Finger Food* ... Some of you camped out last night to get a seat today ...'

The old people in the crowd cheered.

'Go Fiona! Go Bella!'

Zee Zee roared with laughter and hugged his bride while he winked at Bella. Bella's mother looked quite shocked but managed a smile. She had to be on her best behaviour from now on. She had a lot to make up for.

At the wedding party afterwards, Bella tucked into the rose and crystal wedding cake. Through the happy crowd, Fiona approached, with a tall man on her arm. Bella felt her stomach twist at the sight of the familiar face.

'Hello, Ian,' she said, battling to keep the tremor from her voice.

He still had the same twinkle.

Fiona leaned in to whisper in her mother's ear. 'He's a widower, has been for years! Kids live in Australia. How neat is that?' And with a quick kiss on Bella's cheek, Fiona slipped away.

Ian cleared his throat and offered Bella a small object from behind his back.

A small slice of carrot cake with a rose and a crystal on top.

Quick Reads 📖

Fall in love with reading

Why do Golf Balls have Dimples?
Wendy Sadler

Accent Press

Have you ever wondered why golf balls have dimples or why your hair goes frizzy in the rain? Scientist Wendy Sadler has the answers in her book of Weird and Wonderful facts.

Broken down into user-friendly chapters like sport, going out, the great outdoors, food and drink and the downright weird, Wendy's book gives the scientific answers to life's intriguing questions, like why toast always lands butter-side down and why you can't get (too) lost with a satnav.

Quick Reads 📖

Fall in love with reading

Going for Gold

Accent Press

What does it take to go for gold and be the greatest?

In *Going For Gold*, Wales's leading athletes share the secrets of their drive and determination to be the best in their sport.

Cyclist Geraint Thomas, who won Olympic gold in the Team Pursuit in Beijing 2008, and 11 times gold medal-winning paralympic swimmer Dave Roberts talk of their ambitions to win in London 2012.

World champion hurdler David 'Dai' Greene explains his hunger to be the best and the importance of loving what you do, while Commonwealth medal-winning swimmer Jazmin 'Jazz' Carlin and paralympic world champion Nathan Stephens reveal the discipline needed to go for gold.

This collection of stories will inspire others to aim for their goals and follow their dreams.

Quick Reads 📖

Fall in love with reading

Earnie: My Life with Cardiff City
Robert Earnshaw

Accent Press

From the African plains to the Millennium Stadium, this is the remarkable story of the boy who was born to be a Bluebird.

Nicknamed Earnie, this is the story of Robert Earnshaw's journey from the Zambian village where he was born to Caerphilly, where he first kicked a 'proper' football. Seven years later, aged 16, he was signed up by Cardiff City and started banging in the goals on his way to break the Bluebirds' goal-scoring records.

Here Earnie reflects on his Welsh success, his trademark somersault goal celebration and the crazy world of Sam Hammam, and he reveals why Cardiff City will always have a special place in his heart.

About the Author

Born in Llandovery, Helen began her stand-up comedy career at London's Comedy Store. She is best known as the dippy Catriona in the hit TV series *Absolutely Fabulous* with Jennifer Saunders and Joanna Lumley. She has appeared in many hit TV comedies including *Naked Video, French and Saunders, The Young Ones* and *Harry Enfield's Television Programme*. She is a familiar voice on BBC Radio 4. Writing credits include *Coping with Helen Lederer, Single Minding, Girls Night Out* and *Girls Night In*. Her one-woman show Still Crazy was a sell out at the Edinburgh Festival.